Flora the Fairy's Magic Spells

Tony Bradman * Emma Carlow

Reading Ladder

EGMONT

We bring stories to life

Book Band: Green

First published in Great Britain 2009
This Reading Ladder edition published 2016
by Egmont UK Limited
The Yellow Building, 1 Nicholas Road, London W11 4AN
Text copyright © Tony Bradman 2009
Illustrations copyright © Emma Carlow 2009
The author and illustrator have asserted their moral rights
ISBN 978 1 4052 8227 7
www.egmont.co.uk
A CIP catalogue record for this title is available from the British Library.
Printed in Singapore
45877/5

Series consultant: Nikki Gamble

MIX
Paper
FSC   FSC® C018306

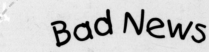

Bad News

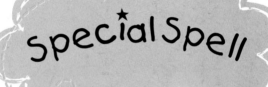

Special Spell

Just Relax

For Oscar and Lily.

T.B.

For my Flora,

up the road.

E.C.

Bad News

Flora the Fairy was really looking

forward to her day at school.

But then she got some bad news . . .

'Good morning, children!' said

Miss Glitter.

'We're going to be busy today.

You have to take a test tomorrow,

so we need to practise for it.'

'What kind of test, miss?' said Harry.

'Oh, nothing too difficult,' said Miss Glitter. 'Just turning Smoky into something, then back to normal.'

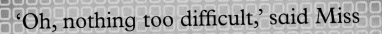

Smoky was their class pet, a baby
dragon. His nest was beside Flora's
table.

'Can we turn him into a dinosaur,

miss?' said Harry. 'Or maybe a shark!'

'No, Harry,' said Miss Glitter with

a sigh. 'OK, let's get on.'

'I'll pass the test, of course,' Harry whispered in Flora's ear. 'My mum and dad will be so proud of me . . .'

I'll be OK.

Flora felt a flutter in her tummy.

She started to worry.

What if she didn't pass the test?
Would Mum and Dad be cross with
her?

Special Spell

Miss Glitter showed them what to do.

But Flora was nervous. What if she

couldn't get it right?

'You wave your wand like this and speak the special spell . . .' said Miss Glitter.

'Spit, spat, spot
– be what you are not!'

There was a loud PING! and suddenly

Smoky was a small unicorn.

Ping!

Wow!

23

'To change him back, you wave your wand and speak a different special spell . . . Spit, spat, spur – be now what you were!'

There was another loud PING! and

Smoky was his old self again.

Phew!

25

'See, it's easy-peasy!' said Miss Glitter.

'Time for you to have a go.'

Most of the children got it right.

But some of them didn't.

Oops!

'Oh, Harry!' Miss Glitter said crossly.

'That won't do at all!'

Everybody laughed at what Harry

had done.

Smoky
doesn't
mind...

Ready, Smoky?

But at least he was doing something, thought Flora.

She tried and tried, but she just kept getting it wrong.

30

'Er . . . spit,
spur, spat . . .'
she said.

'Oh no, spot,
spat, spit . . .'

Finally, Flora burst into tears!

Just Relax

Flora was still sobbing when Dad came to collect her after school.

Miss Glitter had a word with him . . .

and then they flew home.

Mum was there with Nana and
Grandpop.

What's the matter, Flora?

They all wanted to know what was

wrong . . . and Flora told them.

I can't get the spell right.

'Ah, now I understand!'

said Mum.

'But there's no need to worry,' said Dad.

'We could help you practise,'

said Nana.

'That sounds like fun!'

said Grandpop.

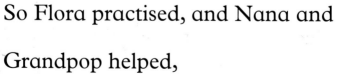

So Flora practised, and Nana and

Grandpop helped,

40

PING!

and Mum and
Dad did too.

After a while
Flora started to
enjoy herself.

41

She changed all sorts of things . . . into

all sorts of other things.

PING!

PING!

PING!

Even poor old Rufus the cat joined in the fun!

PING!

Dad took her to school the next day.

'Just relax,' he said, and gave her a kiss.

'You'll do fine.'

And when she took the test . . . Flora

passed it first time!

Hooray!

'Well done, Flora!' said Miss Glitter.

'Now, if only we could come up with a

special spell to make Harry behave.'

But Flora knew that that was

impossible!

whee!